ANN CHARLES
DEADWOOD
Shorts

SHORT STORIES FROM
THE DEADWOOD MYSTERY SERIES

ISBN: 1940364043
ISBN 13: 9781940364049

Illustrations by C.S. Kunkle
Special thanks to Rebecca Curtis, Genevieve Cushing, and the rest of the CreateSpace team for all of your help building this book!

Dear Reader,

One of the things I've wanted to do since I wrote *Nearly Departed in Deadwood*, the first book in my Deadwood Mystery Series, was to write several short stories that give the backstory of the characters and/or the setting. I chose not to include these bits of backstory in the actual novels because I didn't want to slow the pace.

In this series of short stories, I will offer what I hope to be fun insights to gobble up, kind of like those mini-sized candy bars and MoonPies. Rather than blather on about my random ideas, crazy antics, and diabolical plans, I present to you the first two Deadwood Shorts: *Seeing Trouble* and *Boot Points*.

Seeing Trouble offers answers to some of the questions I've received from fans about how Violet Parker ended up as a single mother of twins.

Boot Points is a collection of short tales about Violet Parker's purple boots. It is set in the story time between the third and fourth book in the Deadwood Mystery series. Each tale not only explains a bit more of Violet's history, but also shows the role each character plays in Violet's life. For this reason, I chose the title of *Boot Points*; because it's not really about the boots ... or is it?

In addition to these short stories, I've included the original character interview I did with Violet prior to writing the first book that introduced us to her wild world and a deleted scene from *Nearly Departed in Deadwood* with an explanation for the scene at its beginning.

I have also included four short stories called *Candy Lover, Dancing with Dialogue, Rainstorms,* and *Metro Madness* that I pulled from my short story vault. These stories have nothing to do with Violet and Deadwood, but they are stories that I felt might put a smile on your face. They were written long before the Deadwood series was born.

I threw in a couple of Deadwood-related illustrations by C.S. Kunkle that were created for my original website. Also, you can see the progression of the cover design for *Nearly Departed in Deadwood*, from the first working cover I created after finishing the first draft of the story, through several contenders drawn by C.S. Kunkle, to the final product that you see today.

I hope you enjoy this compilation of Deadwood Shorts and more.

As Old Man Harvey would say, "Don't squat with your spurs on."

Ann Charles

Ann Charles

P.S.—Special thanks to my wonderful beta readers. I can't say "thank you" enough for all of your time and support. Virtual drinks and cake for all!

For My Wonderful Husband:
Thank you for all of the love and laughter!

DEADWOOD SHORTS

SEEING TROUBLE

Deadwood, South Dakota

"Hey, Mom," said Addy, my nine-year-old daughter, as she burst through my bedroom doorway. "Elvis found this old book in the basement."

She held out a book I hadn't seen in over a decade—my old diary. The upper corner of the cover had been pecked, leaving it tattered.

Elvis was my daughter's pet chicken. Long story short, she planned to save the animal kingdom one pet at a time. Elvis was just another in Addy's long line of birds, mammals, rodents, fish, and amphibious creatures. I'd drawn a line at the garter snake. Indiana Jones wasn't the only one with a loathing for things that go slither in the night ... or day.

"It has a cool little lock on it. It must be a diary," Addy said, holding up a paperclip. "Can I try to pop it open?"

I inspected the lock for scratches, wondering if she already had and was just covering her ass by asking. "You know how diaries work, Addy. They are for the owners' eyes only."

"But we don't know whose diary this is. It could be the long-lost diary of Calamity Jane."

Being that we lived in Deadwood, which was famous for its history of gold rushes and gunfights, my daughter tended to think that anything older than she belonged to some famous historical figure. Take the old rusted spur her twin brother Layne, my very own wanna-be archaeologist, dug up in the yard last week. She was certain it had belonged to Wild Bill Hickok.

"We do know whose diary this is, Addy. It's mine."

"Are you sure? It looks really old."

Shut it, child. "Isn't it time for you to take Elvis for a walk?"

"What did you write about in it?" she asked, ignoring my attempt at distraction.

Your father. "Just some thoughts on life and growing up."

"You should let me read it. I might learn something of value."

It was ironic how whenever she wanted to get her way, she reflected my words of wisdom right back at me. "I'm not falling for that, Adelynn Renee. This book is for my eyes only."

"Come on, Mom," she whined. "Why can't I read it?"

"Because I don't want you to."

In the pages of this little book, I'd written the truth about her father, a man she had yet to meet. I didn't feel like taking a trip down memory lane to visit him tonight with her in tow. It would only raise questions that were better left for after she graduated high school—or maybe college. That asshole of a sperm donor didn't deserve her love and affection before she was able to fully understand what had happened a decade ago.

Addy sighed and threw herself on my bed. "I was hoping we could read it together and bond."

Bond? I narrowed my eyes. "You need to stop watching the Hallmark Channel." I picked up a pair of her pajamas that for some reason were on the floor of *my* bedroom and handed them to her. "Go brush your teeth and climb into bed."

"Ah, Mom."

"Go. Now." I nudged her toward the door. "I'll be in later to kiss you goodnight."

She trudged out the door, her stocking feet sweeping a cluster of dust bunnies with her.

As soon as I heard the bathroom door close, I picked up the diary and popped it open with Addy's paper clip.

Property of Violet Parker

Running my finger over my name, I chewed on my lower lip, remembering. I'd been so young, so clueless. I fanned the pages full of loopy cursive writing. Even my handwriting had been different then—flowing and pretty, not the rushed scrawls I used now.

I stopped on a page with a short, sloppy entry:

July 13th: Crappity crap! I just realized I totally missed my period. It must be the new birth control pills messing with my system. Seems like the nurse said something about this happening. Maybe I should call the doctor.

Ha! If only it had just been the pills making my period a no-show. I'd forgotten all about calling the doctor thanks to the full load of college classes I was taking, my full-time job, and, of course, my preoccupation with Addy's father. His blonde hair, golden brown eyes, and hard body had melted my underwear along with my resistance every time he came around to charm me into bed. I'd had a thing for sexy brainiacs back then, especially a science major who talked like Captain James Tiberius Kirk during sex. Don't ... stop ...Violet.

I flipped a couple of pages, grimacing at the big, bold strokes I'd used on one of them.

July 29th: I'm going to kill her!!! How could she? She knows how much I like him. I hate her. I fucking hate her. I CAN'T BELIEVE SHE SLEPT WITH HIM!!!!

Ah, yes. My little sister, a.k.a. Psycho Susan. I should have known that she was going to be a permanent burr in my ass back when she was four and she cut the hair off all of my Barbie dolls because I'd told her she couldn't play with them while I was at school. Since birth, she'd lived by the motto: What was hers was hers, and what was mine was hers to destroy.

The night I came home early from work and walked in on her naked and gasping in my bed underneath Addy's father was the night I had shut them both out of my life. I still felt a slight kick in my solar plexus whenever the image of them together popped into my head. Her game had sunk to a new level. It was no longer about whom Daddy loved more.

Shaking my head, I flipped forward a few more pages. The writing was short and sweet and slightly smudged.

August 24th: I'm ten weeks pregnant. Shit!

I shook my head, remembering the choking fear squeezing my esophagus when I'd stared at the ultrasound image on the monitor. A baby. Oh, my God, a baby.

My sister had still been hot and heavy with Addy's father at the time. We'd become our own soap opera: The Young and the Pregnant. There had been so much drama in the air that summer, especially the night Addy's dad had come to my door and declared his love for me. When I asked why he was having sex with my sister, he claimed it was only because he couldn't have me.

I tried to break his nose with the door when I slammed it, but he'd been too quick for me.

For the next few weeks, I'd chewed my knuckles about whether to tell him or not about the baby. Maybe he really did love me. Maybe, somehow, we could carve a happy family life out of this mess. Maybe I was delusional from pregnancy hormones.

In the end, Natalie, my best friend, had talked me into giving him a chance to be a father.

I turned the pages until I found the entry about me coming clean with him. Two pages later, I had written down his response.

September 12th: Psycho Susan called me this morning crying hysterically. When she finally calmed down enough to make sense, two words rang clear. "He's gone." So much for having a loving, responsible father for my child. If I ever see the dickhead again, I'm going to tear his nuts off and turn him into a eunuch.

After our little chat about me bearing his child, the jerk never did contact me to tell me I was going to have to fly solo. Apparently, being a genius didn't guarantee he was smart.

A bunch of self-pity filled the next chunk of pages. Then I came across an entry I remembered all too well.

October 5th: TWINS! I'm having twins. Oh! My! God! I'm so screwed. The nurse gave me some information on adoption today after I mentioned that the father had run for the hills, abandoning me to raise two babies on my own. The flyer says that they screen the potential parents, including an FBI background check. I don't know what to do.

I scanned through the next bunch of pages, chuckling at my attempts to return to the dating circuit with a very obvious bump sticking out the front of me. It had been Natalie's idea for me to get out, meet some new men, sniff out a potential father. The only thing I smelled in the dates was a lot of cologne and freakiness.

First, there was the fellow classmate who'd been shocked to learn I was pregnant—he'd just thought I was chubby because I ate like a 300-pound construction worker.

I still wince about the insurance salesman, who after learning why my belly stuck out so far had wanted to cover my baby bump with olive oil and rub his stubble-covered cheeks all over it. Before I shut my apartment door in his face for good, he tried to sell me whole life insurance.

Next came the serious college professor who looked like Magnum P.I. He turned out to be hiding his true age behind dyed hair, a glued-on moustache, and a fake tan. His gray chest hair gave him away, and his desperate fantasy to "bonk" a young female student went unfulfilled by me. My bonking days were long over.

Then there was the angry dentist, the possessed baker, and the narcissistic toy airplane maker. My life had turned into a disturbing nursery rhyme.

Around that time, I finally gave up on men and focused on my new job—Administrative Assistant at a local engineering firm. I decided to keep the babies, much to my family's relief. Well, except for Psycho Susan, who suddenly found the spotlight shining on me and didn't like it that I had toys she couldn't take and mess up—they were attached by umbilical cords.

December 23rd: Got fired today, one week before my probationary period was up. When I asked the HR rep what I did wrong, I was informed that my sister was caught making a pass at my boss when she came to visit me yesterday (I'd been at the doctor's for my monthly checkup and Susan knew it). "What kind of pass?" I'd asked, explaining that my sister was a perpetual flirt. The kind involving her sitting on his lap in a dress sans her underwear. That was probably an accident, I explained straight-faced. Susan sometimes forgot she wasn't wearing underwear—she never has worn them, claiming an allergy to elastic. The HR rep went on to explain that my boss accidentally had his pants down, too. Yikes!

Needless to say, after being told that sisters are usually cut from the same cloth and reminded that I was an unwed mother with no baby-father in sight, I was given a week's severance and asked to pack my things and join my boss at the unemployment office. Susan was at my parents' place when I pulled in the drive. Had I been able to catch her, I might have given her a fat lip. Stupid waddle. She swears he came on to her first, and I think Mom even believes her. Criminy. Who is going to hire an almost 28-week-pregnant mother-to-be? I can't even reach past my belly to the glasses in the kitchen cupboard anymore.

It turned out that the only place that would hire a 28-week-pregnant woman was a 24-hour gas and carryout store. I'd worked there for a full month before my father pulled me aside and begged me to have mercy on him and quit. The stress caused by thinking of his pregnant daughter all alone in a gas station every night had his blood pressure red-lining. I told him that I had to pay rent. He asked me to consider relocating to his basement. He and my mom had talked and agreed they would support me for the first six months of the kids' lives, and then help with babysitting as I got rolling again. My eyes grew misty even now thinking about that conversation with him.

Teary-eyed, I'd told him I'd think about it, which I did three nights later after a red-eyed freak came into the gas station and asked if I needed a foot rub. When I turned him down, he asked if I'd rather practice making another baby. I quit the next morning. My brother moved me back home the following weekend before heading off to the Gobi desert—his next photojournalist gig.

I'd written a lot in my diary during my unemployment. I scanned through lines filled with deep thoughts about the kids, my life, and my aching feet and back. I also plotted revenge schemes, like making a voodoo doll that looked like the sperm donor and backing over it with my car or shaving Susan's head while she slept.

Susan and I had managed to be civil during family dinners, but I stayed in my basement hideout whenever she came to visit the folks.

Mom knew better than to ask me to be the bigger person. I was bigger. I was huge, in fact. But there was no way I could get past the crap Susan had pulled.

As Valentine's Day neared, the thoughts in my diary grew darker, full of worries and anxieties over the two little watermelons that would soon need to be pushed out through a rather small opening in my body. I remember wondering what man would ever want me and my deflated body after the babies had come. Short of rubbing bacon all over my pulse points and wearing barbecued pork-rib earrings, I figured I'd be spending the rest of my life sans men.

February 9th: Cool! I found this small box waiting for me at the table this morning with a card that had my name and a smiley face on it. Inside of the box was a necklace with a daisy pendant. The petals are made of little diamonds and the yellow center is a piece of amber or a yellow sapphire. It looks vintage. I'll have to show it to Aunt Zoe; she's going to love it. She digs this kind of jewelry. Oh, and it came with a matching ring—bonus! Mom and Dad are the best parents ever!

It turned out they were as surprised as I was by the necklace and ring. I asked all around, but the gift giver remained anonymous, everyone in denial. That should have been my first clue. I blame the pregnancy hormones for my stupidity.

I turned the page, knowing what came next, but caught up in the past anyway.

February 14th: Guess where I spent the night, diary? In jail. Happy Valentine's Day to me. That's right, eight months pregnant, and there I sat in a damned jail cell. Granted it was only for a half hour before Mom bailed me out, but still—jail. Why, you ask, my dear diary? Because of my PSYCHO SISTER! What started out with me getting pulled over in my parents' pickup for a taillight being out, turned into the truck being listed as stolen, which then became a VIN record check showing over a thousand dollars-worth *of unpaid parking tickets and fines. To top it off, while I sat at the police station trying to convince them that I had nothing to do with any of this, one of the officers noticed my pretty new necklace and ring and showed me a photo of the very same pieces—reported stolen. Strike three. I went to jail. A half hour later, my mother dragged my sister into the station. She confessed to having reported my parents' truck stolen seven months ago while she was borrowing it for a few weeks. One of her druggy ex-boyfriends had taken off with the truck for days and racked up all kinds of tickets on it. As for the jewelry, they were hand-me-down gifts from her as a way of apologizing for making me lose my job. She'd scored them from another loser boyfriend who'd ripped off a jewelry store weeks ago and bought her affection with them and other sparkly gifts.*

That had been the last entry I'd made in the diary before I had my twins, the last entry period. That night, I'd gotten into a huge fight with Susan. I told her to never come near me again, and then I spilled the beans about something that still makes shame warm my cheeks.

With my stress level through the roof, I'd gone into labor—a month early. Hours later, the doctor pulled Addy out first and then Layne minutes later. I could still hear their teeny, tiny screeches.

Actually, I could hear them now as they fought with each other from opposite sides of the bathroom door.

"Addy!" I yelled loud enough for the tourists down on Deadwood's historic Main Street to hear me. "Let him in to brush his teeth, dang it!"

I looked back at the diary, touching the picture I'd glued onto the page of both of them snuggled together in the little plastic heating bed. I flipped the page and straightened the wrinkled corner of a picture of Natalie—who'd held my hand through it all—snuggling both babies at once, her face split in a huge grin. The next page had a shot of Aunt Zoe leaning over me while I held my babies. She'd stayed with me in the room until I was cleared to go home and promised me that she'd always have room in Deadwood for all of us if we ever wanted to stay with her.

The poor woman, she probably rued that day now that we'd taken over her home.

"Mom?" Addy hollered, the sound of her footsteps coming toward my room.

I closed and locked the book, shoving it under my mattress for safe-keeping before she stepped through the doorway.

"What do you need, Addy?"

She came in and sat on the bed next to me. "I've been wondering something."

"What's that?" I pulled her toward me, tucking her against my side. She smelled like bubble gum flavored toothpaste.

"How old were you when you wrote in that diary?"

"In my twenties."

"Am I in there?"

"Yeah, at the end."

"How come I can't read it?"

I decided to be honest. "Because it takes place during a time in my life when I did something I'm not really proud of."

"You mean getting pregnant with me and Layne?"

"No, Sweetie. It's not that. I'm very proud of you two." When she just stared at me with her golden brown eyes, so like her father's, I explained. "I haven't always been as nice as I am now. "When are you nice?" I poked her in the ribs, making her giggle. When she sobered, she asked, "Were you mean to someone?"

"Yes. Your Aunt Susan."

"What happened?"

"I made her cry."

"How?"

By telling her the family secret—that Dad would never love her like he loved me because she wasn't really his daughter.

"I said something hurtful to her that I can never take back."

"Is that why you two don't ever talk?"

It's part of the reason. "Yes."

Addy was quiet for a moment. "Do you think you'll ever love someone besides my dad?"

I never loved the jerk, but I didn't mention that. "I already have—you and your brother."

"What if my dad came back around and wanted to spend the rest of his life with you? With us?"

I'd probably end up at the Deadwood police station charged with assault and battery. "That's not going to happen, Addy."

She sighed. "Do you think I'll ever find someone to spend my life with?"

"Well, there's Layne."

"He smells."

"And Elvis." Long live the King—or queen in this case.

"Mom, she's a chicken."

"And me."

"Yeah, but you're a smelly chicken." She giggled again. "Will you let me read your diary someday?"

"Yeah, someday."

"Coolio." She hopped off the bed and slid in her stocking feet over to the door. "Elvis is lonely when I'm not home with her. Can we get a pet pig to keep her company?"

Boot Points

Deadwood, South Dakota
Tuesday, 8:20 a.m.

"Elvis, where are my damned boots?" I asked my daughter's pet chicken from the top of the stairs.

Down below, Elvis strutted across the entry hall, her beak jutting with each step. Apparently, she was too busy clucking to herself to give me the time of day.

"Dang bird," I muttered, stomping down the stairs. "You may walk and talk like a chicken, but I swear you're the devil in disguise."

The doorbell rang as I hit the bottom step. Cursing under my breath at the lack of respect Elvis had for me after I'd saved her neck from the chopping block, I yanked open the front door. Doc Nyce stood on the other side of the screen, looking like he hadn't spent his morning wrangling almost-ten-year-old twins, a cat, a gerbil, and a chicken named after the King of Rock n' Roll all while getting razzed by an ornery old codger.

"I can't find my boots," I told Doc as a greeting. I'd been growling and cursing my way around the house for the last twenty minutes, so it took me a moment to take in his white, long-sleeve henley, blue jeans,

16

and whisker-covered chin. *Screeeech!* I did a double take at his ruggedness, my focus zeroing in on his jaw. Damn. No fair. Why couldn't my legs and armpits look that hot covered with stubble?

Touching my hair, I tried to remember if I'd actually combed it this morning.

"Good morning to you, too, Violet," Doc said, pulling open the screen.

He stepped inside my Aunt Zoe's house, where my kids and I were squatting temporarily until I made enough money at my real estate gig to rent my own place in Deadwood. The woodsy scent of his cologne followed him inside and spun my hormones every which way.

"Keep looking at me like that," he said, his dark eyes drinking me up, "and you're going to have to start taking off some clothes before I rip them off."

Balling up my fists, I took a step back before I got burned. What was I doing? Oh, right. "I need my boots."

Doc's gaze headed south, raking down my black, side-slit skirt to my heels. "You're already wearing shoes. Why do you need your boots?"

I waved for him to follow me, escaping the narrow confines of the entryway now filled with testosterone and way too much temptation for an often lonely single mother who was currently the only one home. "I have an appointment today to take my boots in to be fixed."

"You need an appointment to drop off your boots?"

"I want to talk to the cobbler about my options for getting them fixed."

"What's wrong with them?" he asked from behind me.

"Addy's gerbil got loose and used my heel as a tooth sharpener."

"You mean Bogart the gerbil?"

"The gerbil's name is The Duke. Bogart is the cat."

"That's right—Bogart, your vegetarian cat." Doc leaned against the entry arch while I lifted up the sofa cushions and checked underneath. "Which boots are we talking about?"

"My purple ones."

I pulled off the back cushions next and came up empty again. Criminy, where did Addy leave them? Or was it Layne this time? My son had a habit of *borrowing* cylindrical shaped objects and using them as containers. I'd first discovered this when I'd shoved my foot into a boot holding spiral pieces of macaroni destined for Layne's makeshift science lab down in Aunt Zoe's basement.

"I like those boots," Doc said.

"I know." He'd been quite fond of them since I'd worn them the first time we'd screwed around. I tossed the cushions back into place.

"I like you wearing those boots."

"Uh huh." He often called me *Boots* with a twinkle in his eye when he was feeling frisky.

Maybe they'd shoved them under the couch. I kneeled and checked, pulling out a mini baseball bat and a half-eaten sucker stuck back in its wrapper, but no boots.

"I'd like to see you naked while wearing those boots."

I stopped and looked at Doc, who seemed to be very interested in my red silk shirt. "That's not helping me find them." I pushed to my feet.

The twinkle was in his eye. "Maybe we should look for them in your bedroom, Boots."

"Nice try, Romeo," I walked toward him, "but I've already searched there." I'd found dust bunnies, chicken feathers, and a library book on taxidermy, which may have been checked out by either of my kids since one dreamed of being a veterinarian and the other a paleontologist. But no boots.

Doc caught my forearm as I passed him, pulling me up short. "Are you sure you don't want to search it again? This is the first we've been alone in almost a week and you haven't even said 'hello' yet."

"Hello, Doc," I whispered, flushing at the come-hither look in his brown eyes.

He trailed his knuckles along my jaw, lifting my chin as he lowered his mouth.

The mantel clock in the living room clanged the half-hour, slapping me back to my senses. I dodged his lips. "Dane R. Nyce," I chastised, using his full name. "Stop trying to charm me out of my underwear. I have to be at Bighorn Billy's in an hour for a big pow-wow with my coworkers and I can't be late."

It was a bad morning for Harvey to have taken the old pickup I'd been borrowing for a tune-up. Lately, the Picklemobile had been doing a lot of sputtering—well, more than usual—and until I could afford my own set of wheels, the old gal needed some TLC.

"Just to be clear," Doc said, lifting my knuckles to his lips, "could you describe exactly which underwear I am trying to charm you out of? Are we talking lace or satin? The daisy-covered ones or the black ones with the tiny rose sewn on front?"

"You're incorrigible." I slipped free of Doc's grasp before my libido overruled my brain on the case of sex vs. job. "The last thing I need is to stumble into the restaurant with my hair a crazy mess, my lips all puffy and swollen, and a big fat smile that broadcasts I spent my morning doing the wild thing."

"I can't help it." He followed me into the dining room. "Those boots are my kryptonite. Where did you see them last?"

"Addy was wearing them a couple of nights ago while playing Rooster Cogburn."

"Was she Hepburn or the girl?"

"Neither." I peeked under the dining room table. "She was John Wayne. Will you check that coat closet?"

He chuckled, opening the closet door. "That girl follows in her mother's footsteps."

"So I've heard before. I just wish she'd follow in her own shoes instead of in my favorite boots."

"Where did you get those boots, anyway?" he asked, shoving some coats aside, making rustling noises as he searched the closet. "I haven't seen any around here like them."

I shot him a questioning look. "You've been looking for purple cowboy boots? Is this to complete your one-eyed, one-horned, flying purple people eater ensemble?"

"That one's a no-go; my cape is torn," he said, sending me a wink. "I want a pair to keep in my bedroom for those special occasions when Trouble comes calling, wearing her daisy-covered underwear."

That made me smile in spite of my frustrating morning, but I tried not to read more into it relationship-wise than the two of us knocking boots. Doc's last girlfriend had started throwing around the M-word, as in wedding bells and flying rice, and he'd kicked her to the curb like three-day-old road kill.

"Make sure you get size eight with a wide toe," I told him, opening the cupboard doors under Aunt Zoe's antique sideboard. Before my brain could start overanalyzing how often he'd like Trouble to show up on his doorstep, I returned to Doc's earlier question. "Quint bought the boots for me a long time ago."

"Quint, your brother?"

"Yep. They were supposed to cheer me up."

"Why'd you need cheering up?" The rustling noises stopped. Doc was looking at me.

I puffed up my cheeks with a breath and then blew it out, traveling back over the washboard road that wound through my past. I wondered how much I should spill, not wanting him to judge me and find me lacking. Well, more lacking than I found myself most days. In the end, I decided to dump the whole thing out on the floor between us and watch it wriggle and squirm. "Because I'd just found out I was pregnant, and when I told the father, he skipped town before my waistband even got tight."

"He sounds like a real winner."

"My sister, Susan, sure thought so. Did I mention that this happened a few weeks after I'd found out the bastard was having sex with her?" The flash of memory still made my gut clench.

"Are you serious?"

"Unfortunately, I am."

Doc tilted his head to the side, sizing me up for several beats. "That explains a few things."

Huh? "Like what?"

He just shook his head in response. "What did Quint have to say about your sister and your ex?"

What did that explain? Inquiring, crazy inner voices wanted to know. I rounded them all up and shoved them back in their cages.

"He wasn't surprised," I explained. "Susan has always been a wild brat."

Mother's fawning was the result of years of guilt over a glitch in her marriage with my father that ended with having another man's child. While my father had stepped up to the plate to play *Daddy* to Susan, I figured Mom had been trying to ease her guilt by giving Susan whatever the little shit's heart desired. Mom's goal being that Susan would appear to be the perfect child and my father might forget that she didn't share his DNA. Unfortunately, Mom's plan backfired and Susan became a vicious bitch bent on taking whatever was mine and making it hers—including the father of my children. Oh, such happy family memories filled with half-melted Barbie heads and kidnapped favorite teddy bears.

"So, Quint bought you the boots to make you happy." Doc wasn't asking, but I nodded anyway.

"At first he offered to fly home, break Rex's nose, and hang him upside down by his balls."

Doc cringed. "Remind me never to piss off your brother."

I checked under the sideboard in case a child had jammed a boot underneath it, extracting three balled up socks and a pair of scissors.

"But then he settled for having a pair of boots made just for me," I said.

"You said 'fly home.' Where was he?"

"On a job in Mexico." Quint was a photojournalist who was on the road more than home. "He happened to be in León, Guanajuato at the time, working on a piece about famous cathedrals for a magazine, which turned out to be lucky for me since León is nicknamed the 'Shoe Capital of the World.'"

I shut the sideboard door and chewed on my lower lip as I peered around the room. Where could those damned boots have disappeared to?

At Doc's gesture to keep spilling, I continued. "He found this cobbler hand-tooling boots in one of the city's *mercados* and paid the guy a wad of cash on the spot. Two days later, the boots were in Quint's hands. But instead of shipping them, he decided to carry them home with him since he had less than a week left on the job. That's when the problems started."

"You mean with customs?"

"He didn't even make it that far. My brother is a bit of a cheapskate and doesn't always stay in the nicest hotels." Mother often lost sleep while he traveled out of the country. "Two days before he was to fly home, someone broke into his hotel room when he was out and stole the boots."

Doc closed the closet door and leaned against it, listening, one eyebrow raised.

"Quint reported the missing boots to the hotel manager and then headed back to the *mercado* to see if there was any way he could have another pair of purple boots made overnight. When he got to the cobbler's stall, he found the guy's wife there in tears, rattling on in Spanish and gesturing wildly."

"Does your brother speak Spanish?"

"Enough to get him into trouble with a crying woman," I said. "Remember, the whole reason he was even at the *mercado* was because I'd called him in tears."

"Yeah, but you're his sister."

I shrugged. "Quint has always been a sucker for a damsel in distress. Apparently, this woman's husband had a gambling problem and was supposed to have gone the night before to pay back some Mexican bookie what he owed, but he never made it home. She had no idea where he was and couldn't get ahold of him. Quint felt compelled to help, plus he wanted another pair of boots for me. So, he convinced her to close up the shop and then drove her around to the places her husband hung out, including several bars and clubs."

I headed for the kitchen. Doc followed.

"Later that night," I continued with the story, "my dad got a phone call. Quint was in a Mexican jail and needed bail money. He'd been in a fight at one of the clubs. He'd been outnumbered and they'd left him pretty messed up and stolen his wallet."

"Did they ever find the woman's husband?"

"Yes. At the gambling joint where Quint got his ass kicked. The cobbler had either gone there to pay his debt or gamble the money away. But there was a slight problem, which was why Quint was in jail."

"The cobbler was drunk?"

I shook my head. "He was dead with a bullet hole in the middle of his forehead. When the police showed up, they hauled Quint to jail first and asked questions later."

"Christ." Doc sat on the edge of the kitchen table, his arms crossed. "What a mess. All for a pair of boots." When I narrowed my gaze at him, he added, "Albeit some very nice boots, but still."

I started searching through the kitchen cupboards, leaving no bowl unturned. "Quint sat overnight in jail even though Dad had wired the bail money and faxed his identification. The next afternoon, the wife spoke to the police, explaining Quint's role in the whole shebang. They kept the money and let Quint go free after her statement." I pointed at the door on the other side of the table. "Could you check the pantry?"

Doc looked at the pantry door and then back at me. "Why would your boots be in the pantry?"

"Because I have two children."

"Fair enough. So how did you get the boots if the cobbler was dead?" he asked and stepped into the pantry, his broad shoulders filling the doorway.

"When Quint got back to his hotel, the manager pulled him aside. It turned out that one of the maids had brought her daughter to work with her the day before and the girl had taken a shine to my boots. When her mom noticed the boots at home later that evening, the daughter explained that a rich hotel guest who'd felt sorry for her had given them as a gift. But when the alert went out the next day about the stolen boots, the maid forced her daughter to return them immediately and apologized, hoping not to lose her job."

I looked around Aunt Zoe's pale yellow kitchen, my gaze taking in her Betty Boop cookie jar, the drawings of dinosaurs and unicorns taped to her fridge, the sunflower napkins stacked on the lazy susan on the table, the silly chicken pecking at the cat flap Harvey had installed in the basement door. How quickly this place had come to feel like home, even though it was only temporary. I wasn't looking forward to the day we moved on to the next digs, nor my kids moaning and groaning at relocating yet again. But we couldn't mooch off Aunt Zoe forever.

"So your brother risked his neck and sat in a Mexican jail overnight for nothing?"

Crossing to check in the broom cupboard on the other side of the fridge, I told him, "Quint still claims it was great research fodder for an article he later wrote for another magazine about the state of Mexican jails, which won him some fancy journalism award. But yeah, it was all for nothing."

I slammed the broom cupboard door shut. Still no freaking boots. Grrrr. Did Puff the Magic Dragon pop in and out of here, borrowing them without asking me?

"But you got your purple boots," Doc said, shutting the pantry door. "Well, at least one of them, anyway."

I looked over. He was holding one of my boots.

"Where was it? Behind the flour?"

"No. In the corner next to a sack of potatoes." As he spoke, he looked inside of it and then reached in and pulled out a white unicorn with a pink horn.

"Oh," I said, "that's what Addy meant the other night when I tucked her in and she told me Buck was in the hoosegow." Old man Harvey's vocabulary was beginning to rub off on my kids, a fact which made me antsy. It was just a matter of time before a letter came home from a teacher—or I got a call from the principal.

"*Buck?*" Doc frowned down at the unicorn in his hand.

"Yeah, he's one of Addy's favorite stuffed animals. We got him out at Wall Drug."

"But Buck has a pink horn."

I took the unicorn from Doc and placed him on the chair Addy usually sat in for dinner. "You shouldn't judge a unicorn by the color of his horn. Buck is loaded with testosterone, trust me. Now where's my other boot?" I had about thirty minutes and then I'd be officially late to the breakfast meeting.

"Do your kids always ignore normal gender identification cues when naming their pets and toys?"

I shrugged. "They're free spirits—especially Addy. I feel sorry for the guy that falls for her. She's going to take him on one hell of a rollercoaster ride."

"As I said before," Doc ran his fingers over the side of the boot near the pinkie toe, "like mother, like daughter."

25

I was going to ignore his comment, but I couldn't let it go. "Are you trying to say that I'm going too fast for you?" Because if he was, I was going to grab my boot and kick him in the shin after all of the foot dragging I'd been doing in order to keep this thing between us from rocketing out of control—at least on my part.

His eyes held mine for a couple of breaths. I had the feeling he was weighing his answer with care, probably not wanting to lead me on. "No, but you do tend to spin me in loops and steal my breath on sharp turns."

"Oh." Was that a good thing?

"Has your boot always had this scratch?" he changed the subject.

I let him. "Since the kids were babies."

"I guess I didn't notice that before."

"You've been a little distracted when I'm wearing them."

He laughed. "Just a *little*, huh? How'd it get scratched?"

"That's a present from my sister, the bitch from hell."

"Nice nickname. She sounds like a real sweetheart."

"That's just her pseudonym. Her real title is the Bride of Satan."

He laughed again. When I didn't, he sobered. "I take it you haven't forgiven your sister for sleeping with the kids' dad. Or was that moniker earned for scratching your favorite boots?"

"Whether Susan scratched my boots or not was a moot point by then because I already loathed her for so many other reasons."

I took the boot from him, frowning at the scratch and the memories that came with it. I never had understood why Susan hated me so much and with such intensity. Oh, well. I shrugged and set the boot on the floor next to the table. No amount of wishing or wondering was going to change reality, and after putting up with all of her bullshit over the years, I preferred we kept to different hemispheres until death put an end to the whole ugly mess.

"I'm going to go check the basement," I said. "Do you want to come along and keep the spiders at bay?"

"Do you use that line on all of the boys?"

"No, only the ones made of snips and snails and puppy dog tails."
Opening the basement door, I shooed Elvis down the concrete stairs in
front of us. She squawked her opinion of my pushiness. I squawked back
and chased her down a couple of steps. Doc's quiet laughter followed me
down.

At the bottom, I waited for him to join me. When he did, he asked,
"Should I be nervous about being alone with you in a dark basement?"

"Definitely." I hit the light switch on the wall next to us. A line of
fluorescent lights buzzed to life. "You should always be wary of a woman
who wears purple cowboy boots."

"Why's that?"

I didn't have a witty answer, so I shrugged and threw out, "She'll rock
your world."

"It feels more rattled than rocked," Doc said.

Mine felt more like it had been hooked up to a paint can shaker since
I'd tripped over his boxes of books outside his front door.

He followed me over to my son's makeshift science lab in the opposite corner from Elvis's pen—where the bird was supposed to spend her
nights rather than in my closet.

"So did your sister scratch your boot on purpose?" he asked.

"You could say that." I pulled open the deep drawers on an old dresser
Aunt Zoe had relocated down here when we moved in. They were filled
with beakers, measuring cups, and other lab equipment my brother had
bought Layne over the years. "Susan lives to take or destroy anything that
belongs to me."

"You're kidding. She's your sister." After I planted my hands on my
hips and stared at him, he said, "You're not kidding."

There were several crates lined up along the wall. I sifted through
them even though I doubted the boot was in any of them. It was easier to
tell the stories about the kids' dad and my stupidity at that time in my

life without facing Doc. "Unfortunately, I'm not. Take the father of my children. We'd been dating for several weeks when Susan found out about him. She didn't waste any time seducing him and then took great pleasure in letting me know they were having sex—a lot of it—and which positions he liked best."

"That's twisted."

I snorted. "Nah. That's the Bride of Satan for you."

"If she'd already stolen your boyfriend, why did she scratch your boot?"

I flashed back to Susan's screams and waterworks when I'd told her Rex had abandoned me. She'd gone all psycho. For a moment, I'd thought she might actually have been upset about me being left to fend for a baby on my own. How naïve of me. I stacked a couple of the crates, keeping my back to Doc.

"Susan wanted something I had," I explained, "and for once she couldn't get it, so she took her frustration out on my boots."

"Violet, quit being so cryptic."

"You're one to talk," I muttered. Doc was the mayor of Cryptic City, USA, and a pro at dodging my questions.

I dug through another crate full of old baseball mitts, finding one of the sandals I'd been missing for weeks. What in the hell was it doing down here? Then I noticed the toe had been chewed off by something much bigger than a gerbil. What the heck? Had we acquired a dog without me knowing about it?

Doc grabbed me by the shoulders and forced me to face him. "Stand still and tell me what happened."

We didn't have time for me to stand still because the other boot wasn't down here, but I did anyway, handing him my chewed sandal, which he took and tossed back into the crate.

"As I said before, Rex left town when he found out I was pregnant. My guess is that for the next eight months or so, Susan held out hope that he'd return to claim the kids after they were born and the two of them would pick up where they'd left off, only with my children—a happy little family. Remember, she always takes what's mine."

"Yes, the bitch from hell, I got that."

I felt so stupid about my role in the whole soap opera. I closed my eyes to avoid his stare and let the story flow. "After I had the kids, my dad hired a private detective to hunt down their father so my lawyer could send Rex paperwork to sign to revoke all his rights to the kids. The bastard signed off and sent the paperwork back without any hassle, essentially saying goodbye to his children and me. That's when Susan went nuts, getting all up in my face, screaming at me about how I'd ruined everything by driving away the love of her life. She called me all kinds of names, threatened to spend every moment of the rest of her loveless existence destroying mine." God, there'd been so much yelling that day. I tried to laugh at the memory, but it came out brittle, still coated with hurt and anger. "How dare I mess up the wonderful thing she had going with my damned boyfriend, right?"

Doc squeezed my shoulders, comforting me. "What did you do?"

I opened my eyes and locked gazes with him. "I tackled her and tried to strangle her to death." It was not one of my finer moments in life.

He laughed. At my flat stare, his grin flipped into a frown. "You're serious?"

"Yeah, I am. It took my father and mother both to pull me off of her that day." I sighed, remembering those hate-filled days and silent family dinners, and then pushed onward with the foul explanation. "Our house was pretty tense for a while. Susan was pissed at me for driving Rex off and at my dad for making sure Rex wouldn't return to screw up my life more. After a week of that, Mom asked me to bring my babies up here to Aunt Zoe's place for the weekend. While I was here, Susan packed up her shit. When I returned, Susan was gone and so were my boots."

His eyes narrowed. "She didn't."

"Oh, she did, and I'm sure she was smiling wide when she took them from my closet. Susan knew how much I liked them, what they represented, and all that Quint had done to get them for me."

"What a bitch."

"From hell," I added with a wry grin.

"How'd you get the boots back? Did you hunt her down?"

"Not quite. You see, she didn't just move across town, she moved across the country—south, down to New Mexico."

"She kidnapped your boots and left the state?"

I nodded.

"Don't tell me she tried to hold them for ransom."

"No, she never intended to give them back, but then someone changed her mind."

"Your parents?"

I shook my head. "Natalie."

"Natalie? Was she friends with Susan?"

A laugh erupted from my throat. "Hell, no. I think Nat hates her more than I do." If that was possible. "When Nat found out about Susan taking my boots, she took a road trip."

"Natalie drove to New Mexico just to get your boots back?" He stepped back, his tone filled with incredulity.

"It was never about the boots for Nat. It went way deeper, starting with some rumors that Susan had spread when we were in junior high. Nat doesn't forgive and forget easily, and she refuses to let something go once she sinks her teeth into it."

"She sounds like she's part badger." Doc caught my hand, just holding it. His touch felt warm, comforting, making me want to lean into him for more, but I held back.

"When the whole sex thing with Rex and Susan happened," I continued, "Nat wanted to go all Tasmanian Devil on them, but I made her promise to drop it. I just wanted to be free of them and move on with my life. But when Susan stole my boots, that was the final straw, and no matter what I said, Nat was hell bent for leather."

Purple leather. I thought back to the fury that had contorted Nat's face when I told her the boots were gone. "Since Susan slinked off into the night, Nat had to track her down. She started with the address for Rex, who had moved to Texas and was working for some research facility there. When Nat met up with Rex, he admitted that he'd recently talked to my sister, but only to tell Susan to stay away from him. He figured my sister was there to try to get some money from him to help me."

"I'm surprised he was willing to talk to Natalie about any of this."

I shrugged. "Nat can be pretty convincing, especially while wielding a pair of pliers and a crowbar."

Doc cringed.

"Rex spilled that Susan was living in Santa Fe, New Mexico. That was where Nat found her, working at an art gallery, wearing my damned boots."

"Did Natalie use the pliers on her?"

"I wish. Susan took off running as soon as she caught sight of Nat, who still laughs about the whole scene. She described my sister as 'a gazelle fleeing across the savannah.' Unfortunately for Susan, Nat can sprint like a freaking cheetah. She was a track star in high school. Nat tackled her in an alley and tore the boots off Susan's feet, leaving my sister with a black eye and a warning to stay away from me and my kids."

Susan had abided by that threat for a few years, but then had showed up again on my parents' doorstep, back for more money and to wreak further havoc. But there was no need to go into that now. We had a boot to find.

I stepped around the lab table, glancing one last time around the basement for any sight of purple. "The scratch is Natalie's fault, according to Susan," I wrapped up the story, "who swore the boots had been in pristine shape until Natalie tackled her in that alley."

The image of Nat waltzing into the car dealership where I'd worked at the time and handing me back my boots made me grin.

"Is your life always this chaotic, Trouble?" Doc asked, leaning against the workbench abutting the wall next to the crates. He glanced down at the papers on Layne's desk and did a double take.

"Of course." I backed toward the stairs, watching a frown crease his forehead. "I'm a single mom with twins."

"Hold on a second." He held up two pieces of paper. "I think these are plans on burial extraction and a map of gravesites."

I paused at the bottom step. "I'm not surprised. Layne thinks this house was built over an old horse graveyard." I pointed at the sheets of paper. "Put those down and come on."

He let the papers drop onto the bench. "Are you sure Layne's thinking about animals here?"

"Ninety percent sure, yes. We talked about this a couple of weeks ago at dinner. He knows the rule—he can only dig up animals. No humans."

After one last glance at the papers, Doc walked toward me. "What kind of scientist is his father?"

"I don't remember. Something super brainiac and unbelievably boring."

He chuckled. "And yet you managed to get pregnant by him."

I glared down at him. "He was tall, handsome, and charming. It seems I have a certain weakness around men who fit those criteria."

Stopping two steps below me, Doc stood almost eye level with me. "Are you saying I'm smart and boring, too?"

I faked a yawn. "Well, you make up for it in the sack."

"Vixen," he growled and reached for me, but I dodged his hand and raced up the stairs with him chasing my behind. When we reached the kitchen, I grabbed the single boot and held it out toward him like a sword.

"Stay back. We have a boot to find."

He grabbed the boot from me and pulled me close, dropping a soft kiss on my lips, his tongue tasting and teasing at the same time.

The need for more—much more—lingered long after he pulled away. How was a girl supposed to play hard to get around him, damn it?

"Now where?" he asked.

"I don't know. I already searched all over upstairs." I looked back toward the living room, chewing on my lip. Where had I missed? The attic? Surely they hadn't taken the boot up there. I'd even checked Aunt Zoe's room. Where else could it ...

Oh! "Aunt Zoe's workshop." I grabbed the key from the key rack near the back door.

The air outside chilled my bare arms. The scent of cinnamon greeted us inside the cool workshop thanks to an air freshener that almost hid the usual smell of the kiln. Dust floated in the shaft of morning sunlight shining through the window over Aunt Zoe's work sink.

Closing the door behind Doc, I said, "If you don't mind looking around out here, I'll check in back."

I found nothing in Aunt Zoe's storage room. When I returned to the front, I found Doc staring at a picture of me that Aunt Zoe had slid into the bottom corner of an old mirror hung on her wall.

"How old is this picture?" Doc asked.

I checked inside the cupboard under one of her work counters. "I don't know, maybe six years or so."

"You're wearing your purple boots in it."

"Actually if you look closer, I'm wearing a boot bracelet with these gorgeous glass and metal charms that Aunt Zoe made just for my purple boots." I walked over next to him and plucked the picture from the mirror, looking down at the photo Aunt Zoe had taken of me one summer day long ago. In it, I was leaning back on the lounge chair with my boot in the air, posing like some fashion model. The kids had been standing just outside of the shot giggling like mad. I could still hear their laughter in my head. "She told me it was supposed to bring me good fortune."

"Did it?"

"I lost it before it had a chance to pay off." I stuffed the picture back into the mirror. "She made me another one that looked a lot like that one, but I refused to wear it on my boots again—I didn't want to lose it. I keep it in my jewelry box now, along with some of the stuff she's made for Addy and Layne."

"More charm bracelets?"

"No. For Layne, she makes him these bookmarks with charms on the tassel. He uses them in the books he's always carrying around. Addy gets wrist and ankle bracelets and necklaces. Aunt Zoe makes Quint little good luck charms, too. He's supposed to carry them with him at all times." I hadn't ever paid attention to whether she made them for Susan.

"I wouldn't have pegged your aunt as the superstitious type."

"I know." Aunt Zoe was usually the salt-of-the-earth type of mentality. But every now and then she surprised me.

"What's with this mirror?" Doc tapped on it.

"It reflects light."

"Not very well, smartass." He poked my ribs, making me laugh and wiggle away.

"What do you mean?"

"All of the corners are getting foggy and the frame is all dented and scratched. What kind of metal is that?" He brushed the pads of his fingers over it, then scraped down it. "Some kind of bronze?"

I hadn't really thought much about it before; it just had always been in the workshop. "I guess."

"There are some weird symbols on it."

"I think they're Latin symbols." Checking my watch, I glanced at the door. We really didn't have time to play Indiana Jones right now.

"Are you sure?" Doc asked, not picking up on the ants in my pants. "I've seen plenty of Latin symbols over the years while researching but not these. Not before now. Not even in that old book you 'borrowed' from the Carhart house."

"Well, I thought Aunt Zoe told me they were Latin, but I could be wrong." I walked over to the door and held it wide. "She said they have something to do with protecting those who look into it."

"Protecting from what?" He stared at me in the fog-edged mirror.

I shrugged. "From going out in public with something in your teeth, I guess." I jutted my chin toward the house. "You ready?"

"Each side a unique piece," he said under his breath, then touched the left upper corner. "Did your aunt weld this together?"

Why on earth was he suddenly so interested in that mirror? "I don't know. I never asked. It's pretty old, though."

"How old?"

"Like old-old." When he looked at me with a wrinkled brow, I added, "I don't know when it was made, but it's been in our family for a few generations, I think. I know that Aunt Zoe's had it for as long as I've been around." A fuzzy memory formed. "Quint once asked her about it when we were kids. She told him that our grandmother had given it to her and made her promise to keep it safe from harm."

That wasn't all she'd said. My thoughts returned to that day a long, long time ago. When Quint had asked if he could have it when he grew up, Aunt Zoe had shaken her head. *This is not for you, Quint.* Then she'd looked over at me.

Why can't I have it? Quint had asked, his eight-year-old voice tinged with a whine.

Because you're a boy, Aunt Zoe had explained, patting him on the arm. *Only the girls in our family have the strength to use it without letting it change us.*

At the time I'd thought she was picking on Quint, but Aunt Zoe had reinforced that the mirror was mine repeatedly over the years, keeping only my picture on it, as if to tether the mirror to me.

The neighbor's dog barked, snapping me back to the present. "You ready to go back inside?" I asked Doc.

He gave the mirror one last glance before joining me outside, waiting as I locked up the shop. "Where to now, Nancy Drew?" he asked.

"I don't know. We're running out of hiding places."

His cellphone rang. Pulling it from his pocket, he said, "It's your bodyguard," and took the call without breaking stride. "Harvey."

When we reached the back porch, Doc paused with one foot on the bottom step. "Really?" he said into the phone, then looked up at me, his brow creasing. "Yeah, I'm with her right now." Another pause. "No, at her aunt's place, looking for boots."

I heard Harvey say something and then Doc laughed. "Not knocking boots, looking for them."

I shook my head. Knowing Harvey as I did, I highly suspected the dirty old bird had heard Doc just fine.

"She can't find her purple pair," he explained. "Well, one of them, anyway." There was a flurry of noise from Harvey's end, then Doc held the phone away from his mouth. "Harvey wants to know if you've looked in the laundry room. He saw one of your boots in there on the shelf next to the soap last night."

Old man Harvey had been spending a lot of nights on my Aunt Zoe's couch, so much so that he was starting to bring his laundry with him. He claimed that he was keeping an eye on me after all of the trouble I'd had lately with some of Deadwood's more frightening citizens, but I wondered if any of it had to do with the body parts his old yellow dog kept digging up on his ranch. I certainly wouldn't want to be hanging around there after dark, especially with those freaky folks just down the winding dirt road in Slagton, a mining ghost town that went "sour" years ago according to locals. Just last week Harvey had told me he'd found a favorite hat that had been missing for months nailed to a STOP sign three miles back toward the creepy town. It had been filled with bullet holes.

Just thinking about that again gave me the chills. Maybe I should be acting as Harvey's bodyguard instead of the other way around.

"Why didn't he say something about the boot to me then?" I asked, switching back to the present.

"What's that, Harvey?" Doc listened to the phone again while watching me. A grin creased his cheeks. "He said there was a pair of pink flowery skivvies—his word, not mine—stuffed in the boot. He would have washed them but was afraid he'd get your cooties if he touched them."

Cooties? Harvey had definitely been hanging around my kids too much.

"So he looked inside of the boot," I said, "and then just put it back on the shelf with my underwear still crammed in it?"

Doc repeated my question through the phone. He listened for a moment. "He says it's not his business where you keep your boots," he stopped to listen again, adding, "or your skivvies."

Holding the phone away from his face, Doc covered the microphone with his thumb. "On a side note, I'm happy to make the location of both your boots and skivvies my personal business."

I playfully pinched his forearm. "You tell that ol' buzzard ..." I hesitated, remembering that Harvey currently was taking the Picklemobile in to get it looked at after having taken my kids to school. Not to mention that he'd cooked us all breakfast this morning and grilled hamburgers for dinner last night.

"Tell him what?" Doc asked.

"You tell him that I appreciate his help," I finished, then mentioned for Doc's benefit, "I'm going to go check the shelf in the laundry room."

I'd reached the back door when Doc's voice stopped me. "Violet, Harvey said if you find the other boot, leave them on the back porch and he'll stop by and take them to get fixed for you."

As sweet as the gesture was, I knew better than to assume he'd do this out of the goodness of his crusty old heart. I pursed my lips. "At what cost?"

Doc repeated my question and then let out a loud laugh.

I didn't wait around to hear Harvey's answer, tugging open the screen door and slipping inside the kitchen. I made a left turn into the laundry room. I'd already checked in here once, but hadn't looked higher than eye level. Sure enough, the boot was up on the top shelf. Whichever kid had stashed it here must have stood on the dryer to get it up there. I went up on my tiptoes and grabbed it, pulling the flowered panties out of it.

"I haven't seen those before now," Doc said from the doorway. "Is there a matching bra?"

I tossed the underwear into the dirty clothes basket. "Not a bra, a camisole."

"Love those, too." He took the boot from me. "Mystery solved, Miss Drew." He inspected where the gerbil had sharpened its teeth. "The whole heel may need to be replaced." He looked over the rest of the sole. "It's pretty worn. I noticed the sole is cracked on the other one."

"Sounds like me." After years of struggling to raise two kids on my own, worn and cracked could describe the face of the monster staring back at me in the mirror each morning.

Doc lowered the boot. "You think you're cracked?"

"Maybe." *Definitely.* But that wasn't something I needed to broadcast to the guy I wanted to see a lot more of in the near future. Crazy-assed women make scary bedfellows—wasn't that a saying somewhere? Maybe it was a Harvey-ism. Dear God, I'd been hanging around the ornery old coot too much.

"Why do you think you're cracked?"

"I haven't had two good nights' sleep in a row in weeks. Between all of the nightmares I've been having and Detective Cooper breathing down my neck most days, Mr. Sandman has started avoiding my bedroom like I've been quarantined." I rubbed the back of my neck. "He's probably afraid Cooper's going to arrest him, too," I added with a grimace.

"Detective Cooper is just trying to protect you."

"He sure has a funny way of showing it, barking at me through the fence every other day."

"He's a cop. He's wired to sniff out danger and bark at it, and 'Trouble' is your middle name."

I wrinkled my nose at Doc. "Well, Cooper should try walking a mile in my boots and see if he doesn't step in some shit along the way."

"They'd cramp his toes." Doc grabbed me by the elbow and led me back into the kitchen. "And his style."

"What style?" I scoffed and took the boot from Doc. "You mean his bullet-hole T-shirts and neckties with little handcuffs covering them?"

"I was thinking more along the lines of him only seeing things in black and white, while you are looking through purple-tinted lenses."

"Are those like rose-colored glasses?"

"No." He pulled me into his arms and I went without a fight. "Your vision is definitely purple." He tipped my chin up and brushed his lips across my forehead. "Ultra-Violet, even," he added with a small smile before kissing me more thoroughly.

I let the boots dangle and then slip from my grip, wrapping my arms around his neck, plastering myself against the front of him like a windbreaker in a stiff breeze.

He pulled back.

"What was that?" I asked, still breathing heavily.

"That was a proper hello kiss, Boots." His eyes had that twinkle again. "You sure you can't spare ten minutes before we have to head out the door?" His lips trailed along my jawline, his hands exploring my contours through my shirt.

"Ten minutes isn't enough."

"Is that a challenge?" His hands pulled my hips tight against him as he backed me up against the counter.

"No, not a challenge. I just want longer than ten minutes with you."

"But then you'll be late," he said.

"I'll tell them I had pickup trouble." I tugged him into the dining room.

"Your hair will be messed up."

"From being so frustrated with that damned pickup."

"Your lips will be swollen."

"I'll hide behind my coffee cup." I started up the stairs. "Wait! My boots."

He came up behind me. "Don't worry about your boots. I'll take them in to get fixed today after I drop you off."

I smiled down at him. "You'd do that for me?"

"Of course. Just tell me exactly what you want done with them so I can explain to the folks at the boot place." He stood eye level with me, his hands framing my waist. "I have big plans for you and your boots, you know."

I wasn't sure what that meant and at the moment didn't feel like thinking too much about it. I slid my arms around his neck. "What about right now?"

"I have big plans for right now, too, but we're short on time, so we'd better get moving." He nudged his chin toward the top of the stairs.

"I mean don't you want me to wear the boots right now?"

"There's no time for that. Besides, I don't know if you realize it," he said softly, his eyes darkening as he stared at my mouth. "But it's not really about the boots, Violet."

The End ... for now

DEADWOOD
EXTRAS

INTERVIEW OF
VIOLET PARKER

Following is an interview I had with Violet Parker before I began writing *Nearly Departed in Deadwood*. Sometimes I interview several of my characters, sometimes just one. For this book, since I was going to be solely in Violet's head, I only interviewed her.

Enjoy,
Ann

———————•———————

Tin Cup Café in Deadwood, SD
The morning sunshine has just crested the tree-covered hills overlooking Main Street, lighting the red brick road in an orange glow, creeping through the coffee shop's front door. The air drifting through the open door still holds a breath of coolness, the sun's rays haven't heated the sidewalk to a boil yet. From the radio perched on the shelf over the bottles of

flavored coffee syrups, Eric Clapton is singing *Willie and the Hand Jive* on the local station.

The smell of steamed coffee beans makes my mouth water. Unfortunately, they don't have any soy milk on hand, so I'm shit-out-of-luck when it comes to a flavored latte. A big, burly axe-swinging type of a guy lumbers by me on the way to the counter, the century-old, scuffed wood floor creaks under his feet. In his wake, my Diet Coke can wobbles on the small, round table where I sit waiting for Violet Parker to join me.

I shift on the hard, wrought iron seat again, sip some soda pop, and check my cell phone for the time—Violet is fifteen minutes late. She wanted to be at the office by 9 a.m, so our scheduled meeting time of 8 a.m. *should have* given us just enough time to get acquainted.

I glance out the window. Not many tourists line the sidewalks yet, mostly retirees who are up early to gamble away some of their pensions and fast-walking, uniformed folk obviously on their way to work. The espresso maker steams loudly, hissing over Clapton's swanky tale about Way-Out Willie.

A curly-haired blonde appears in the doorway, pausing to scan the room. I recognize Violet's face from her picture on Calamity Jane Realty's website and wave at her. Her tight smile and wrinkled brow show a mixture of frustration and tension as she approaches. Then I notice the child-sized blue handprint on the shoulder of her pale pink blouse and I can't help but chuckle.

Me: Is that paint?

Violet: (She drops into the chair opposite of me.) Is what paint?

Me: The blue handprint on your shoulder.

Violet: (She looks down at her shoulder and the furrows in her brow deepen.) Oh, shit (she says under her breath as she brushes at the blue print, which merely spreads further across her shoulder). Nope, it's chalk, compliments of my son.

Me: Let me buy you a coffee.

Violet: (*Still smudging the chalk around on her shoulder*) I would love a caramel latte, but you don't have to buy it for me.

Me: I owe you one for letting me interview you. I'll be right back. (By the time I return to the table with her steaming latte, she's given up on the blue smudge and is holding her cell phone up in the air.) Here you go (I set it down in front of her).

Violet: I need a new provider. (*She snaps her phone closed.*) What good is a Realtor whose phone gets a signal only when she's standing on top of Terry Peak?

Me: How's the realty business treating you these days?

Violet: (*Her grin twists at the corners.*) I'd be better off selling encyclopedias. Thanks for the coffee (*she sips from the steaming cup*).

Me: How many houses have you sold so far?

Violet: A big, fat zero.

Me: How long have you been working for Calamity Jane Realty?

Violet: Two and a half months. And in that time, I haven't had a single bite. I've shown a handful of clients a vacation house or two, but nobody has signed any offer letters. And if I don't land a deal soon, I'm going to be out on my ass.

Me: What do you mean?

Violet: Jane, the owner, took me on as a favor to my Aunt Zoe with the deal that I had to make a sale within the first three months or she'd have to let me go. She can't afford to carry me if I'm not bringing in any money.

Me: What will you do if she lets you go?

Violet: I don't know. I could try to get my old job back, but I don't want to work with those jerks at the car dealership any more. And I hate being tied to that place for five days a week, plus every other weekend. Being a Realtor has been so much more freeing. I can have lunch with my kids in the park, or take them to doctor's appointments in the middle of the day. They seem so much happier since we moved out of Rapid City.

Me: You're living with your Aunt currently, right?

Violet: Unfortunately.

Me: Don't you get along with her?

Violet: Oh, yes, Aunt Zoe is wonderful. She's happy to share her house with me and the kids—at least that's what she keeps telling me. It's just that I hate mooching off her so much. She lets us stay in her house for free. She won't even take money for a portion of the bills. The most I can do to repay her is keep the cupboards full, which is getting harder and harder with Layne's ever growing stomach.

Me: Is Zoe retired?

Violet: No, she owns and runs the art gallery just up the street. She creates her own glass designs and sells them for an insanely cheap price. She could get four times as much if she wanted, but she insists that her art is for the average American pocketbook. She says there is more money in selling to the masses than the elite, especially in Deadwood, although she does have this deal going right now with an art gallery in Denver. The gallery's owner visited Deadwood last year and stopped in at Zoe's place. He was so impressed with her work that he wants to display and sell her stuff in his gallery. She's hard pressed right now to finish the last four pieces of the twenty he requested by the end of this month.

Me: I'll have to go check out her gallery while I'm in town. So, tell me about your kids.

Violet: (She smiles and grabs her purse, pulling a couple of pictures from her wallet.) This is Adelynn—but she insists on being called Addy. (She shows me a picture of an adorable little blonde holding up what looks like a long, green ribbon toward the camera.)

Me: She likes ribbons?

Violet: Ribbons? (*She looks down at the picture.*) Oh no, that's a dead snake.

Me: Eww.

Violet: Yeah, I know. She's really into animals—alive and dead. She wants to be a veterinarian when she grows up. Aunt Zoe thinks Addy should be a taxidermist since she has no problem handling dead things. (*She holds another picture out.*) And this is Layne, Addy's twin brother.

Me: Twins, huh? (I stare down at the picture of another cute face surrounded by dark blond hair. The boy has Violet's hazel eyes.)

Violet: Yep, born a few minutes apart. Addy came first, so she considers herself Layne's "older" sister. She takes care of Layne, from picking out his clothes some days to making his lunch for school every morning. Not that Layne likes her choice in clothes or healthy foods.

Me: And what does Layne like to do when he's not in school?

Violet: (*She stuffs the pictures back into her purse.*) This summer, he's learning Spanish with Mona.

Me: Really?

Violet: Yes. He wants to be an archeologist, and he's set his sights on South America.

Me: Wow. How old is he?

Violet: They both turned nine last month.

Me: That's ambitious for a nine year old.

Violet: He's watched *Raiders of the Lost Ark* too many times. My dad loves that movie. He and Layne watch one of the three movies from the Indiana Jones series every time they're together.

Me: Who is Mona?

Violet: She's another Realtor at the office. She wants to retire in Mexico in a few years—her sister lives down there and runs a property management company for vacation homes on the beach. Mona bought some learn-Spanish software, and she and Layne are practicing together. She adores my kids, the crazy woman.

Me: Where do your parents live?

Violet: Down in Rapid City.

Me: Was it hard to move away from them?

Violet: Not really. My mom has been pressuring me to date a guy from the neighborhood for the last year. He's about seven years older than me and is pretty good looking, but he's about as exciting as a snail race. Mom often had Ed "joining us" for dinner. I actually folded to Mom's will this last winter and went on a date with Ed. Biggest mistake I could have made. Mom started talking about wedding dresses and reception halls. I could feel the world closing in around me. That's when I saw a billboard for a Realtor school and decided to get out of the rut I'd been spinning my tires in and take a chance on something new and exciting. The kids were game in spite of having to leave their school and friends behind. They have always loved visiting Aunt Zoe and the idea of living up here in the hills seemed pretty romantic to them.

Me: And here you are.

Violet: Yep, here we are. (*She swallowed a gulp of coffee, and then her lips curled into a smirk.*) And if I don't make a sale in the next couple of weeks, we'll be on our way up shit creek.

Me: Do you like working at Calamity Jane Realty?

Violet: For the most part. Mona is great and Jane is nice. But then there's Ray ...

Me: What's wrong with Ray?

Violet: If there was an award for the World's Biggest Horse's Ass, Ray's walls would be lined with first-place plaques. He's an egotist drowning in "old-boy" mentality, and he has it in for me.

Me: Why?

Violet: Because his nephew is going to school to be a Realtor and Ray wanted him to get the job that Jane gave to me. He is counting the days until the end of the month and the end of my job.

Me: Sounds like a fun guy to work with.

Violet: One week with him and you'd be ready to stab a number 2 pencil in his eye and pray he dies a slow death from lead—well, graphite—poisoning. Natalie wants me to spike his coffee with arsenic, but I don't know where I can buy arsenic these days.

Me: Who's Natalie?

Violet: She's a good friend of mine. She grew up here in Deadwood. I'd hang out with her every summer when I came to stay with Aunt Zoe for a month or so while I was growing up.

Me: What does Natalie do?

Violet: Natalie does a lot of things—she's a dabbler. She dabbles in photography, carpentry, astrology, and the male sex. For money, she is the caretaker for a private campground and lodge just outside of town. She's a jack-of-all-trades.

Me: Sounds like someone else I know named Claire Morgan—especially the campground caretaking bit.

Violet: I know a girl named Claire Morgan. She's Natalie's cousin. Her family lives next to my parent's place. She was in the grade below me. I played kick-the-can with Claire and her younger sister, Kate, all of the time. (She chuckles and swallows the last of her coffee.) Their older sister, Veronica, always insisted we wear reflective vests when we played. How are you supposed to sneak up and kick the can when you stand out like a freaking runway beacon?

Me: Yep, that's Claire and her sisters. It's a small world.

Violet: Especially in the Black Hills. Do you have the time?

Me: (I look down at my cell phone.) It's eight-forty.

Violet: (She grabs her purse and stands.) I'm sorry to cut this short, but I should head to the office. I want to get in before Ray brews a pot of coffee this morning.

Me: You found a place that sells arsenic?

Violet: (She winks.) Something like that. Thanks for the latte.

Me: You're welcome.

Violet: (She pauses at the door and smiles back at me.) Don't be a stranger.

Me: Oh, I won't.

DELETED SCENE FROM
NEARLY DEPARTED IN
DEADWOOD

Following is a scene that was in the original version of *Nearly Departed in Deadwood*. In this original version of the story, in addition to Violet having a secret admirer, she also had a stalker. This stalker was the result of one of Addy's attempts to find a husband for Violet. The stalker kept calling, leaving threatening-sounding messages on Aunt Zoe's answering machine. He coerced Violet to meet him for a "blind" date at Hardee's restaurant in Rapid City by mentioning that he knew where she lived. So, Violet agreed to meet him for a meal, and old man Harvey went along as backup, with the promise that he'd wait in the Bronco for Violet and "watch her back."

Without further ado, here is the deleted scene.

"This place is dead," Harvey said as I swung my rig into the Hardee's parking lot.

"Good." It would be easier for him to play Peeping Tom.

"Why are you parking here, girl?" he asked as I pulled up next to the only other vehicle in the lot—a rusted Ford van, windowless in the back. "I'm gonna need some space to get off a clear shot."

"Harvey, I told you, there will be no shooting tonight." I shut off the engine and nailed him with a glare.

Halfway down to Rapid City, Harvey mentioned that he'd forgotten to pack the slugs. Having lead pellets dug out of my skin was not how I wanted to end my night.

Harvey crossed his arms over his chest with a *hrumpf!* His lower lip jutted. "Then how do you expect me to save your ass? Hit him with a round of harsh words?"

I tossed him my cell phone. "Three numbers: nine, one, one." Before he could argue with me anymore, I shoved open my door and hopped to the ground.

My tennis shoes felt springy on the asphalt after clomping around in mule-heels all day. The pavement still oozed heat. On the western horizon, the early evening sunshine held steady above the Black Hills, shrouding their eastern-facing slopes with dark shadows. Down here on the prairie, it was easy to see how the hills had earned their name.

Like any fast-food joint worth its salt, Hardee's smelled of French fries and greasy burgers. I'd have been drooling if I wasn't about to meet the man who'd spent the last two weeks harassing Aunt Zoe's answering machine. As it was, the aroma of sizzling fat had me gulping back the nausea bullying its way up my esophagus.

Ignoring the imploring stare of the uniformed high school kid standing behind the register, I scanned the dining room. The cheery notes of Bobby McFerrin's *Don't Worry, Be Happy* rang through ceiling speakers. I growled at the irony.

A pair of well-rounded, middle-aged lovebirds occupied one of the center tables, sharing a heap of fries and a bounty of adoring gazes. Fast food and romance—an odd combination, but who was I to judge? As a single mom who'd had sex just once in over two years—and that was only by accident—I had a lot to learn about affairs of the heart.

In a booth in the back corner, a rail of a guy sat hunched over a foil-wrapped sandwich. On the table across from him, a large drink, a bag of fries, and an unopened sandwich were laid out picture-perfect on a tray. Martha Stewart would have been proud. As I stared, he looked up at me from behind a pair of owl-eyed glasses and smiled.

Bachelor number one, at my service.

My heart bucking like a pissed-off bronco, I crossed the tiled floor. My soles made a ripping sound on the sticky spots.

"Hi," my voice trembled. I cleared my throat and tried again. "I'm Violet."

His glasses magnified the size of his eyeballs, making his irises extra big and extra hazel. Up close, I noticed the thin, blonde moustache furring his upper lip. As if he'd suddenly remembered his manners, he scrambled to his feet, almost knocking over his drink in the process.

"I'm Gary." After stabilizing his cup, he held out his hand. His palm was softer than the skin on my kids' tummies. "I'm glad you could make it."

I dropped into the booth seat across from him, lining up with the place setting he'd laid out for me. "You didn't give me much choice."

He smiled, apparently missing the barb in my words. His teeth were straight, except for one crooked canine. "He was right."

"Who was right?"

"Dr. Schmirnof."

"Schmirnoff? As in the vodka?"

"Yes, but that has two F's. Dr. Schmirnof was my cellmate."

Cellmate? Oh, crap. "You were in prison?"

"Of course. You knew that. Or didn't you read my comments on your profile page?"

"Profile page?" I was playing parrot again, but I couldn't help it. Crazy shit was flying at me way too fast.

"On FeloniousLove.com."

Jeez! I was going to lock Addy in Aunt Zoe's basement when I got home and not let her out until she was eighteen. That damned 'ex-cons seeking true love' website she'd placed me on weeks ago was coming back to bite me in the ass. "So, you didn't read my singles ad in the paper?"

"I can't afford the newspaper yet." Gary reached across the table, placed his hand over mine, and squeezed, comforting. "It sounds like you're a very lonely woman, Violet. I hope I can help you."

I doubted it—unless he had a house to sell. I pulled my hand free, hiding it under the table. "Your cellmate—"

"Dr. Schmirnof."

"You mentioned that he was right. About what?"

Gary reached into a black backpack on the seat next to him. I would have bolted if my feet hadn't turned to stone. Expecting a knife or gun or rocket launcher, I did a double take when he pulled out a book and laid it on the table between us. I stared down at a man who looked like a twin of Jerry Garcia, tie-dyed shirt and all. Printed across his forehead were the words, *Don't Take No for an Answer!*

"What's this?" I asked, leaning over it.

"It's a dating guide for shy people—like me."

"A dating guide?"

"Yes." Gary flipped open the book to a dog-eared page. "See. Right here in Chapter Six, it says you should be aggressive, call several times a day to show how much you really want to see the person, and find out where they live so you can have flowers delivered."

My chin hit the table. "You mean to tell me that all of this stalking business has been something a dating guide told you to do?"

"Stalking?" His big eyes grew even larger, filling his face. "I haven't been stalking. Just showing I'm interested."

Now was not the time to argue semantics. Our food was getting cold, and now that it looked like I wasn't going to be hauled away, tied to a chair, gagged, videotaped, and tortured, my stomach was trying to chew its way to the surface. I plucked a soggy French fry from the bag on my serving tray. "What were you in prison for, Gary?"

"An accounting discrepancy."

"Addition errors get you five-to-ten these days?"

"When you're working for the wrong group of guys it can."

Ah. I stuffed the fry in my mouth. It was cold and chewy, tasted like stale potatoes, but I didn't care. "So, does this book recommend having first dates in fast-food restaurants?"

His cheeks turned pink. "I'm a little tight on cash. My assets are still frozen."

"Gotcha." I sat back, swallowing the fry along with a gaggle of hysterical laughs trying to escape.

"Would you excuse me for a minute, Violet? I need to use the restroom. I was a bit nervous waiting for you and it appears I drank too much."

"Sure."

"You won't leave, will you?"

"No way." A free meal was a free meal.

"I'll be back before you know it." He scuttled off.

Two more fries followed the first. As I waited for him to return, I plotted more ways to torture my daughter and came up with some real winners come prom age.

"Hello, Violet."

In the middle of swallowing another fry, I choked at the sound of Doc's voice. Pieces of processed potato slipped into my nasal passage, making my eyes burn and water. Doc needed to quit showing up unannounced and discombobulating my throat muscles.

After sucking down some ice water from the cup in front of me, I squinted up at Doc. He still wore his red T-shirt and blue jeans. "What in the hell are you doing here?"

"You didn't call about Jeff's place."

"I forgot." I'd been too busy trying to sneak a peek into Ray's desk all afternoon in between running petty errands for Jane. Unfortunately, the only thing I found besides the ordinary desk-drawer paraphernalia was a Rec Center Programs' schedule. While this piece of evidence had a possible tie-in to the pool, it wasn't exactly a bloody knife.

His lips thinned. "You forgot to call me, or you forgot to call Jeff?"

"Both. Sorry." I slunk down in the booth, feeling like a five-inch stiletto heel for not following through on my words. Then I remembered what day it was. "Hey, aren't you supposed to be at Natalie's right now?"

"I rescheduled."

"Why?"

"Something came up."

"What?"

His stare pegged me to the seat cushions. "You."

"What's that supposed to mean?"

"You figure it out." He dropped onto the bench next to me and hip-checked me into the wall. "Harvey said to tell you to stand up while you eat. He can't see you through the bushes."

"Why doesn't he move?"

"He said it's too hot to sit outside. He's got your Bronco idling with all the vents aimed at him."

"My air conditioner isn't working." It had released a loud rattle and a dying gasp on the way to pick up Harvey this afternoon, and then blustered hot air at me no matter how many times I kicked the panel. I could only imagine how expensive it would be to fix it. As if I didn't have enough bills gobbling up my meager savings with Addy's emergency room visit.

"Yeah. Harvey's pretty pissed about that." Doc stole one of my fries. "Yuck, this is cold."

"Ummm, hello?" Gary was back, hovering and frowning.

Doc looked up, his grin appearing. He held out his hand toward Gary. "Howdy. Are you the guy who's been calling Violet?"

"Uhh, yes." Gary shook Doc's hand. "I'm Gary."

"Nice to meet you, Gary." Doc waved toward the opposite booth seat. "Please, join us."

"Who are you?" Gary asked as he sat down across from us.

"I'm Doc, Violet's fiancé."

I choked on another fry.

VERY SHORT STORIES

FROM THE ANN CHARLES' VAULT...

Candy Lover

A Very Short Story from the Ann Charles' Vault

"I want a lover," Candy announced.

Larry nearly choked on his corndog.

Candy pushed a strand of ash-blonde hair out of her face and tipped her head to the side, her expression thoughtful. "Someone who will accept me for who I am."

She stared across the midway at an old man leading his wife toward the grand stand and sighed. The hot afternoon sunlight reflected off the pool half-full of floating rubber ducks next to her balloon-dart carnival booth, the rays shimmering on her smooth, tan cheeks.

Larry wiped the back of his hand across his mouth and frowned at Candy. "You're pregnant."

Candy grinned at him. "Only seven months."

Adjusting the straps of her dark pink sundress, she focused on the two teenagers who'd stepped up to her counter. Their fingers were entwined, their gazes starry, as if cupid had just knocked their heads together. Candy handed the boy three darts.

A drop of sweat rolled down the middle of Larry's back as he watched the kid throw the first dart. Moving up next to Candy, Larry reached for her as she wavered on her feet. He needed to buy a couple of fans for her. The summer heat roiling off the blacktop couldn't be good for her or the baby.

He helped her sit on the stool next to the helium tank. "Sweetheart, you're so pregnant you can't even see your own shoelaces," he said for her ears only.

Pop! Pop! Pop! The kid nailed three balloons.

"Winner winner, chicken dinner!" Candy called out.

The kid's girlfriend squealed and clapped, pointing at the green stuffed frog hanging on the wall.

Candy used Larry's shoulder to push herself up on her feet again. "Yeah, but some men find pregnant women attractive, don't they?" she asked, grabbing a broom handle with a hook at the end. The frog fell after two nudges. Larry bent down and picked up the frog for her. She took it and handed it to the young girl, watching with an almost wistful smile as the kids walked away, arms around each other, hands in each other's back pockets.

When Larry moved to her side, she looked up at him and asked again, "Don't they, Larry?"

Larry shifted under the weight of her gaze. The gold flecks circling her brown irises seemed to sparkle in the sunlight, mesmerizing him. The heat roiling from the blacktop in front of her booth knocked him back a step. He pulled a rag from his pants pocket and wiped the sweat off his neck.

Across the way, a group of young boys eyed his fake rifles. Maybe it was time to return to his shooting range booth. "I s'pose some do, Candy."

"Then how hard can it be for me to find a lover?"

Grimacing, Larry said, "Why now? Why can't you wait for a couple of more months?"

"Months?" Candy laughed and nudged him with her hip. The smell of her raspberry-scented shampoo mixed with the sweet aroma of Candy made him gulp.

"Come on, Larry," she said, rubbing her hand over her round stomach. Her eyelashes looked white-blonde in the sunlight. "Do you think that just because I'm pregnant I don't want to have sex? That I don't miss being in a man's arms, waking up next to someone, being touched and stroked until I howl at the moon? I may be pregnant, but I'm not dead."

Touched and stroked ... Damn, he didn't want to think about Candy and sex in the same sentence—not about kissing the smooth, silky skin stretched across her swollen stomach; and definitely not about touching her full, round breasts that were cresting the top of her sundress. He needed to get away from her before he did something stupid that fucked up their friendship.

"Listen, Candy, your sex life is none of my business, but I don't think it would be good for your bab—"

"Never mind, Larry," Candy cut him off and turned her back on him. She waddled over to the helium tank and pulled a balloon out of her pocket.

Larry shrugged, hopped over her counter, and cut through the crowd to his booth.

"Damned woman," he muttered and hurdled his own counter.

He'd known Candy for four months now. He'd watched her blossom from a slender, cute girl into a lush, curvy woman. The asshole who'd knocked her up had been a carnie, too, but he'd left the company before Larry had signed on. What kind of a piece of shit would leave Candy and their baby all alone and never even look back?

Larry had kept to himself the first few weeks on the job, pretending not to notice Candy's tears that fell only when she thought nobody was watching. But then one evening the soft tinkling sound of her laugh had drawn him across the walkway to see what had her so tickled. Later that evening, long after he'd felt the baby moving under her skin, she'd asked him to sit with her outside of her camper and watch the meteor shower. He'd surprised himself by agreeing.

The next week, she'd come over to his counter carrying an elephant ear and split it with him, wiping the powdered sugar off his beard stubble when they finished.

The week after that, he'd offered to drive her to her doctor's appointments. She'd insisted on cooking him breakfast in return as payment. No mortal man could resist her homemade blueberry pancakes, especially when served with her double dimpled-smile.

The sun slipped behind a cloud and Larry glanced over at Candy's booth. His gaze locked on a slick-dressed, leather vested hotshot with greased-back hair leaning on Candy's counter. Whatever the shithead was saying had those dimples showing.

Bile burned his throat. What was wrong with her, flirting so obviously, so wantonly? Where was her pride? He kicked at the shotgun closest to him and knocked it off its holder.

Larry turned away from the two of them. Like he'd said before, Candy's sex life wasn't his business, nor did he have time to watch out for her if she was going to pursue this finding-a-lover bullshit. Besides, he had a booth to run for the next few months until the season ended. After that, he had to fly home to reality, where the day-to-day stress of running his family's construction company made him pop antacids like Tic-Tacs.

Why should he care who she screws?

He pulled his emergency half-empty pack of cigarettes from the shelf under the counter and tapped one into his hand. He'd quit smoking when he'd tagged his brother to take his place running the family business and signed on as a traveling carnie. Until today, he hadn't felt the need to light up. He wasn't even sure where he'd left his lighter.

Candy giggled again, the soft sound enticing his glance her way. His gut twisted. The son of a bitch had his lips on her wrist.

Dragging his eyes away, he stared down at the cigarette in his hand. Why did he care so much about who she had sex with? His mind drifted, imagining what it would be like to peel off her sundress one strap at a time, to see the sweat glistening on her ripe body, to touch...

Oh, God, he had to think of something else, like the subcontractors who always came in twenty percent over estimate, or delivery trucks that never showed up on time, and inspectors who wanted something under the table before they'd give their approval.

He paced across his booth and back. The damned woman had to be ten years his junior. He had no business thinking of her as more than the friend she'd become, more than a woman about to bring a child into this world on her own with no man to help.

His gaze snuck back across to where she stood, fanning herself under the sun's rays.

The memory of sitting next to her on her counter weeks ago while sharing a bag of doughnut holes played through his thoughts. She'd smelled like the vanilla milkshake she'd spilled down her mini-dress, her laughter infectious. When she leaned back on her palms and her dress inched up her legs, he'd noticed how the freckles on her thigh formed a "C." The urge to trace the letter and then explore what else she was hiding under her dress had sucked all of his breath from his lungs. He'd launched himself off the counter so fast, he'd practically fallen on his ass at her feet.

Across the way, the asshole tugged Candy down to whisper in her ear, her breasts threatening to fall out of her dress. Her sweet giggle scraped over Larry's nerves.

"No fucking way is this going to happen," he said and threw the cigarette down. Vaulting over his counter, he plowed through the crowd and yanked Candy's arm away from the asshole's grip.

He climbed over her counter and stood in front of her, the rapid rise and fall of his chest had nothing to do with the afternoon heat.

Candy looked up at him, her eyes narrowing. "What are you doing, Larry?"

"You've found him," he said and pulled her close. Her hard stomach rubbed against his, her shoulders soft and smooth under his palms. Cupping her face, he lowered his mouth to hers, starting off slow, gentle, afraid of hurting her.

But then she wrapped her arms around his neck and kissed him back, frenzied and hard, moaning his name against his lips.

"Candy," he groaned and fed the need that had grown with each passing day he'd watched her blossom, each shared laugh, each brush of her skin against his. Jesus, she tasted so damned sweet.

When he lifted his lips and looked into those golden-lashed eyes, Candy grinned up at him. "What took you so damned long?"

DANCING WITH DIALOGUE

Years ago in a creative writing class in college, we were given the assignment of writing a short story using dialogue only—no narrative elements allowed, not even the dialogue tags that tells who is saying what. This was a fun challenge for me, and you can see from my short dialogue-only story below, *Dancing with Dialogue*, that I was dabbling in romance long before I wrote about Violet Parker's crazy love life.

"Should I ask Joyce out?"

"That's something you should run by one of your guy friends, not me."

"Who do you think I should ask to dance tonight? The brunette in the hot-pants or the redhead in the mini-skirt?"

"The brunette keeps rubbing all over Mr. Cowboy Hat."

"Good point. The redhead it is."

"You do realize she's narcissistic."

"How can you tell?"

"She watches herself dance in the mirror."

"Dang, you're right. Who should I dance with then?"

"Don't ask me. I don't know your type."

"Bullshit. How long have we been friends?"

"Too long."

"What's with the attitude tonight?"

"Nothing."

"Spill it."

"There's nothing to spill."

"That biker dude over by the bar keeps staring at you."

"That's his problem."

"Why don't you go get us some drinks?"

"I'm not thirsty."

"A little flirting might cheer you up."

"I'm not in the mood to flirt."

"That's too bad. You look really good in those boots."

"Shut up."

"When you walked out wearing that dress, my mouth went dry."

"Since when do you pay attention to what I wear?"

"With you, I pay attention to a lot. I bet you could snare any guy in here you wanted tonight."

"Any? You're wrong."

"Prove it."

"There's no need."

"Because I'm right."

"No, you're not."

"Then prove me wrong."

"I already have."

"What's that supposed to mean?"

"Think about it."

"I don't get it."

"I know. That's been the problem since we met. I can't stand this any longer. Here's a ten for my drink."

"Where are you going?"

"Anywhere else."

"Wait!"

"I'm tired of waiting. Let go of me."

"No, I'm not letting go. Not now. Don't leave me."

"You'll be fine without me."

"I won't."

"Why not?"

"I don't want to ask Joyce out. I never did."

"Great. You don't need my help after all. Now, let go."

"And I didn't want to dance with the brunette or the redhead."

"So, why did you even drag me here tonight?"

"Dance with me."

RAINSTORMS

Rainstorms was an experiment using a metaphor as a vehicle to tell a story. At the time I wrote it, I did not have any children, but I had watched my sisters raise their kids almost singlehandedly while balancing jobs and life. Just the bits of babysitting I did for them gave me a small taste of the insanity that can develop over years of parenthood. Now, after having my own kids and balancing a full-time day job and life, the following short story seems quite normal. In fact, I should probably go buy some more dog food.

The first time it rained cats and dogs, I ran around trying to catch them before they hit the ground.

The baby's screams had drowned out the thunder, and the mountain of dirty clothes had blocked out the light, so I couldn't see the building storm clouds through the laundry room windows. Joey kept jumping off his bed onto the floor above me, so I didn't think anything of the flickering 60-watt light bulb over my head or the distant dull thuds when the first few animals hit the roof.

As I climbed the stairs with a basketful of folded clothes, Janey's heavy-metal heartthrob blared through the hall and drowned out everything with screeching guitars. I stepped into her room to yell at her to turn down the music and an orange tabby bounced off her bedroom window, following by a brown and white beagle.

I screamed and threw the basket. Clothes flew everywhere. Janey squealed in surprise and turned down the music. The pounding on the roof reverberated through my skull. I raced down the stairs, out the front door, and made a diving catch for a Doberman Pincher.

The second time it rained cats and dogs, I dragged all of our mattresses out onto the front lawn and hid under the kitchen table. The baby had been teething that morning, and Joey had found the artist within himself. He was busy using the white living room walls as his canvas and his Crayola markers as his medium. I had just found a joint in the front pocket of a pair of Janey's dirty jeans when I heard the first thump.

The third time, Joey was practicing going potty like a big boy on the living room floor and Janey interrupted me while I was in the midst of scrubbing the carpet to ask about birth control. First came a bang, then a meow, and then a wiener dog landed on the hood of my minivan. I stood staring out the front door watching as animals dropped from the sky.

The fourth time, my husband had just told me that he lost $20,000 of our savings at the horse track. This time I left bowls of dog and cat food out along the driveway and wore earplugs.

Now I grow catnip in the flowerbeds and leave fifty pound bags of dog biscuits on the front porch. I don't notice the rainstorms so much these days, just the extra cats and dogs hanging around the neighborhood.

I took a part-time job to escape from home a few nights a week. My husband takes care of the kids when I work. Last night after work, when I crawled into bed and shut off the light, he turned to me in the moonlight and whispered. "Did you see anything strange falling from the sky tonight?"

I pulled the cover up over my head and giggled.

METRO MADNESS

I chose to include this final short story because it shows the mixture of paranormal and humor that I was developing back before Violet Parker sprung to life in my head. As a side note, I was riding the city bus at the time, so I can thank King County Metro for the inspiration for this story.

I'm sorry to say that my college professor was not thrilled with how I kept dabbling in the genre fiction world with all of my odd short stories. I have a feeling he thought I wasn't taking his homework assignments seriously. Little did he know that what I was doing all of those years ago was practicing with different fictional elements, which I would someday compile and use in various full length novels. I was honing my skills, experimenting like a mad scientist with different combinations to create a fun mixed-genre story—aka the Deadwood Mystery Series.

⁎

My bus driver is a vampire, but nobody believes me.

Not even my sister, who rides the bus with me every day. She tells me that I need to seek help. I told her that I have consulted a higher authority on the subject, but she does not feel that my Magic Eight Ball counts.

So, a week ago I decided to prove it to her.

On Monday, I held my compact mirror up in the front of his face. He frowned at me and asked me to sit down.

On Tuesday, I wore a necklace of garlic under my sweatshirt and sat right behind him. He opened his window and told me to move back a few seats.

On Wednesday, I sprayed him with a squirt gun filled with holy water. He bellowed and confiscated my squirt gun, and then advised my sister to remove me from his sight as quickly as possible.

On Thursday, I carried a wooden stake and showed it to him. He threatened to take me to the police station.

Today, I pressed a cross I made with popsicle sticks against his forehead. He slammed on the brakes and kicked me off his bus.

Now, as the bus rolls past me, I wave at my sister, but she is too busy hiding behind her book to see me. I decide to walk to the next bus stop and wait. Oh, well, vampire or not, he definitely needs to work on his anger management.

Pulling out my phone, I dial my sister's cell phone.

"Yes?" she says. I can hear the squeaking and rattling of our bus in the background.

"I guess he's not a vampire after all," I tell her.

"Did you take your pills today?"

"Let's catch the earlier bus Monday morning," I say and hang up.

On Monday, we climb on the bus, show our passes to the driver, and then take a seat on the right—our lucky side.

My sister pulls a book out of her briefcase and begins to read. I lean my head back and stare at the driver as we bounce along.

Three stops later, my sister lowers her book and looks at me. "Please tell me you're not going to start with the vampire thing again."

I smile at her. "No. I don't believe in vampires anymore."

"Thank God!" She raises her book.

I lean over and whisper, "But did you notice all of the hair in the driver's ears? I wonder how he feels about silver bullets and full moons?"

DEADWOOD
COVERS AND
ADDITIONAL
ARTWORK

The Beginning of the Deadwood Mystery Series

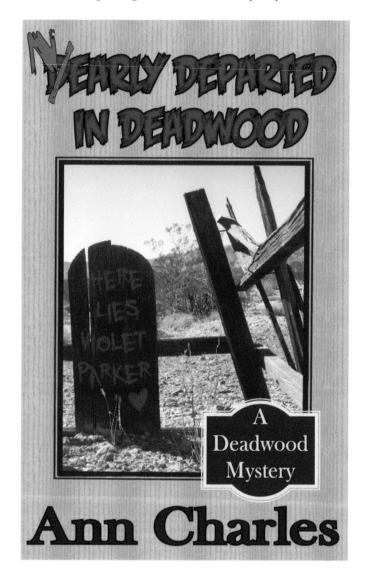

First Cover Attempt - Nearly Departed in Deadwood

Nearly Departed in Deadwood Cover – Contender #1

Illustration: C.S. Kunkle

Nearly Departed in Deadwood Cover – Contender #2

Illustration: C.S. Kunkle

Nearly Departed in Deadwood Cover – Contender #3

Illustration: C.S. Kunkle

Nearly Departed in Deadwood – ARC Cover

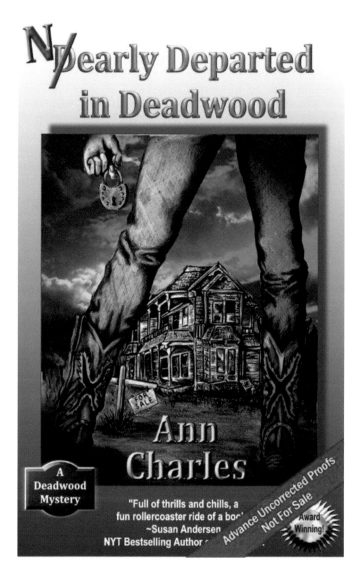

Illustration: C.S. Kunkle

Nearly Departed in Deadwood – Final Cover

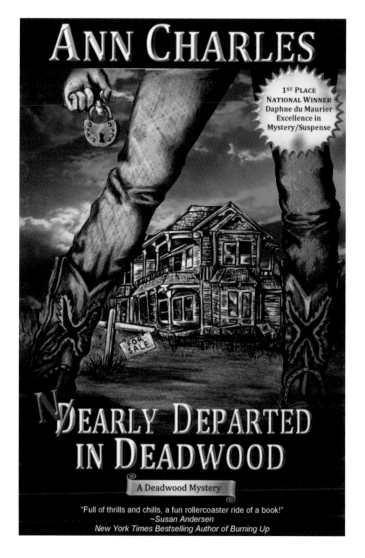

Illustration: C.S. Kunkle,
Cover Design: Kathy Thomas and Mona Weiss

Boney Wild Bill for Ann's Deadwood webpage

Illustration: C.S. Kunkle

Street View of the Historic Homestake Opera House (Used in the Fourth Book in the Deadwood Mystery Series: Better Off Dead in Deadwood*)*

The Bullock Hotel in Deadwood by C.S. Kunkle

The Hessler House - for Ann's Deadwood webpage

Illustration: C.S. Kunkle

Bloody Mistletoe from Nearly Departed in Deadwood *by*
C.S. Kunkle

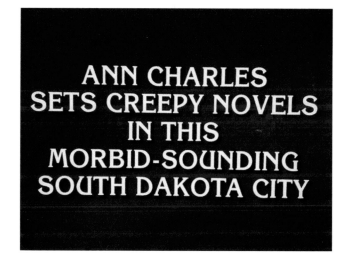

Thanks to the Jeopardy crew for including
my Deadwood Series in 2012.

Ann's Bookends by C.S. Kunkle

ABOUT THE AUTHOR

Ann Charles is an award-winning author who writes mysteries that are splashed with humor and romance and whatever else she feels like throwing into the mix. When she is not dabbling in fiction, arm-wrestling with her children, attempting to seduce her husband, or arguing with her sassy cat, she is daydreaming of lounging poolside at a fancy resort with a blended margarita in one hand and a great book in the other.

Connect with Me Online

Facebook (Personal Page): http://www.facebook.com/ann.charles.author
Facebook (Author Page): http://www.facebook.com/pages/Ann-Charles
Twitter (as Ann W. Charles): http://twitter.com/AnnWCharles
Twitter (as Deadwood Violet): http://twitter.com/DeadwoodViolet
My Main Website: http://www.anncharles.com
My Deadwood Website: http://www.anncharles.com/deadwood

Also by Ann Charles

Nearly Departed in Deadwood
(Deadwood Mystery Series - Book 1)

Optical Delusions in Deadwood
(Deadwood Mystery Series - Book 2)

Dead Case in Deadwood
(Deadwood Mystery Series - Book 3)

Better Off Dead in Deadwood
(Deadwood Mystery Series - Book 4)

Dance of the Winnebagos
(Jackrabbit Junction Mystery Series - Book 1)

Jackrabbit Junction Jitters
(Jackrabbit Junction Mystery Series - Book 2)

Short Stories
The Old Man's Back in Town
(from the Goldwash Mystery Series)

Coming Next from Ann Charles
The Great Jackalope Stampede
(Jackrabbit Junction Mystery Series - Book 3)

An Ex to Grind in Deadwood
(Deadwood Mystery Series - Book 5)

If I Fall You're Going Down with Me
(Goldwash Mystery Series - Book 1)

CPSIA information can be obtained
at www.ICGtesting.com
Printed in the USA
LVIC04n2119180115
423392LV00001B/1

9 7 8 1 9 4 0 3 6 4 0 4 9